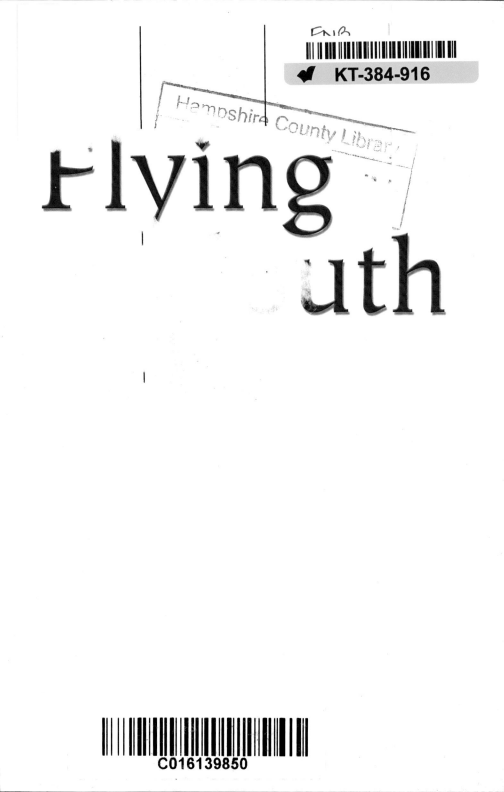

Flying

uth

ReadZone Books Limited

First published in this edition 2015

© in this edition ReadZone Books Limited 2015
© in text Alan Durant 2005
© in illustrations Kath Lucas 2005

Alan Durant has asserted his right under the Copyright Designs
and Patents Act 1988 to be identified as the author of this work.

Kath Lucas has asserted her right under the Copyright Designs
and Patents Act 1988 to be identified as the illustrator of this work.

British Library Cataloguing in Publication Data (CIP) is available
for this title.

Printed in Malta by Melita Press.

ISBN 978 1 78322 410 4

Visit our website: www.readzonebooks.com

Flying South

by Alan Durant

illustrated by Kath Lucas

It was raining.
Bird was wet.

"I'm fed up with this!"
cried Bird. "I'm flying
south to find the sun."

Flap, flap, away she flew...

7

...until the rain ended.

8

"Hooray! I'm south!" said Bird.

9

Bump! Thump!
Hail stones hit her on the head!
"I'm fed up with this,"
said Bird.

Flap, flap, away she flew...

...until the hail ended.

"Hooray! I'm south!" cried Bird.

13

Flutter, flutter, snowflakes fell.

"Brrr! I'm fed up with this,"
said Bird.
Flap, flap, away she flew…

...until the snow ended.

"Hooray! I'm south!" cried Bird.

Whoosh!

A great wind blew her into the air on and on…

...until the wind ended.

"Hooray! I'm south!" cried Bird.

The sun shone.

23

It was too hot.

"I'm fed up with this!" cried Bird.
Flap, flap, away she flew.

She flew and she flew…

27

...until she was home again!

And it was raining.

"Lovely," said Bird.

Did you enjoy this book?

Look out for more *Magpies* titles –
fun stories in 150 words

The Clumsy Cow by Julia Moffat and Lisa Williams
ISBN 978 1 78322 157 8

The Disappearing Cheese by Paul Harrison and Ruth Rivers
ISBN 978 1 78322 470 8

Flying South by Alan Durant and Kath Lucas
ISBN 978 1 78322 410 4

Fred and Finn by Madeline Goodey and Mike Gordon
ISBN 978 1 78322 411 1

Growl! by Vivian French and Tim Archbold
ISBN 978 1 78322 412 8

I Wish I Was an Alien by Vivian French and Lisa Williams
ISBN 978 1 78322 413 5

Lovely, Lovely Pirate Gold by Scoular Anderson
ISBN 978 1 78322 206 3

Pet to School Day by Hilary Robinson and Tim Archbold
ISBN 978 1 78322 471 5

Tall Tilly by Jillian Powell and Tim Archbold
ISBN 978 1 78322 414 2

Terry the Flying Turtle by Anna Wilson and Mike Gordon
ISBN 978 1 78322 415 9

Too Small by Kay Woodward and Deborah van de Leijgraaf
ISBN 978 1 78322 156 1

Turn Off the Telly by Charlie Gardner and Barbara Nascimbeni
ISBN 978 1 78322 158 5